Todd's Teacher

by Janelle Cherrington • illustrations by Ben Hodson

Illustrations previously published in *Tyler's Teacher* by Anne Patton, illustrated by Ben Hodson. Published by Scholastic Canada Ltd.

Text copyright © 2009 by Scholastic Inc.
Illustrations copyright © 2006 by Scholastic Canada Ltd.

ISBN-13: 978-0-545-16152-7
ISBN-10: 0-545-16152-5

12 13 14   40   18 17

SCHOLASTIC INC.

New York • Toronto • London • Auckland • Sydney
Mexico City • New Delhi • Hong Kong • Buenos Aires

Todd loved his school.
He loved his teacher.
Her name was Ms. Cole.

Ms. Cole made Todd feel smart.
"Good job!" she said.

Ms. Cole made Todd feel fast.
"Good job, Todd!" she said.

Ms. Cole made Todd feel brave.
"You did it," she said.

Todd loved his school.
He loved his teacher.
He told his mom.
He told his dad.

But his dad had big news.
It was time to move!
It was time for Todd
to move to a new school!

"I will not move," Todd said.

"I will stay at this school.
I love this school.
I love my teacher.
I will ride my bike to school," Todd said.

"It's too far to ride your bike," Mom said.

Todd went to school.

"You look sad," Ms. Cole said.

"I have to move," Todd said.
"I will not feel smart
in a new school."

"Yes, you will.
You **are** smart, Todd,"
Ms. Cole said.
"And you work hard."

"I will not feel fast
in a new school," Todd said.

"You will.
You **are** fast, Todd," Ms. Cole said.

"You are brave, too," she said.

"But you will not
be my teacher," Todd said.
"So I will not be brave."

"You do not need me, Todd.
You are smart.
You are fast.
You are brave
all on your own," Ms. Cole said.

Ms. Cole gave Todd a hug.
Ms. Cole made Todd feel happy.

Now Todd was all set to go
to a new school!